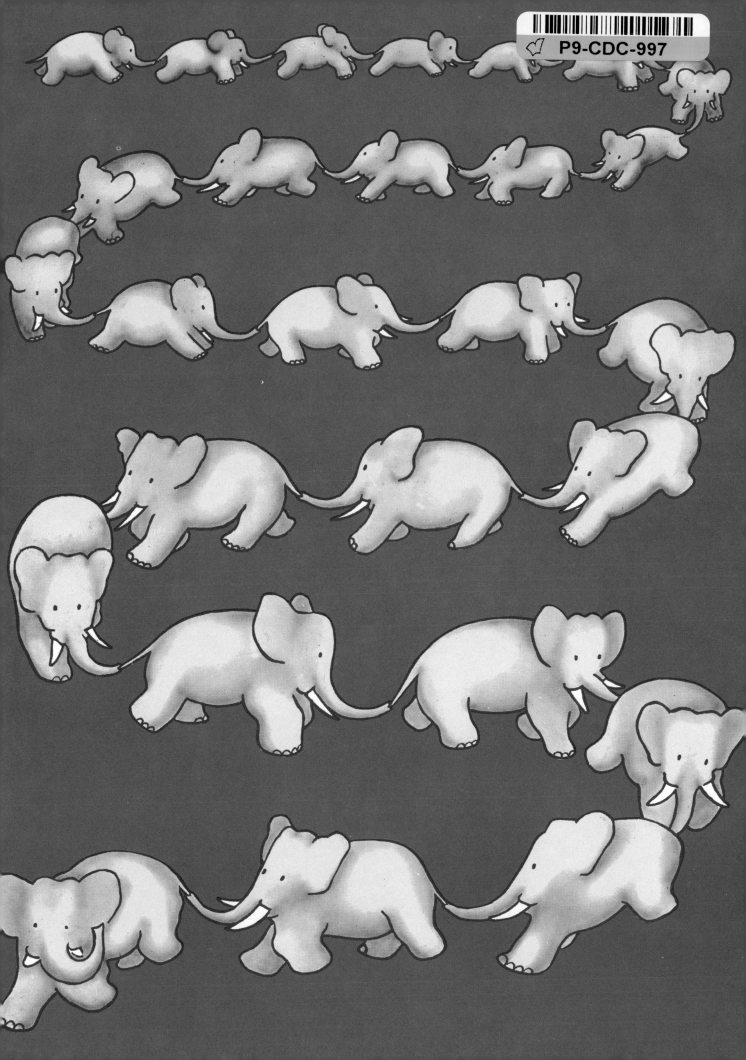

JEAN DE BRUNHOFF

BABAR
THE KING

Translated from the French by Merle S. Haas
Random House — New York

Babar Books
Babar and Father Christmas
Babar and Father Christmas (facsimile of original edition)
Babar and His Children
Babar and the Professor
Babar and the Wully-Wully
Babar and Zephir
Babar the King
Babar the King (facsimile of original edition)
Babar Visits Another Planet
Babar's ABC
Babar's Anniversary Album
Babar's Book of Color
Babar's Counting Book
Babar's Fair
Babar's French Lessons
Babar's Mystery
The Story of Babar
The Story of Babar (facsimile of original edition)
The Travels of Babar
The Travels of Babar (facsimile of original edition)
Babar's Little Girl

Pictureback® Paperbacks
Babar Learns to Cook
Babar Saves the Day
Meet Babar and His Family

Little Boxed Sets
Babar's Bookmobile
Babar's Little Library
Babar's Trunk

Beginner Books
Babar Loses His Crown

Deluxe Coloring Books
Babar's Coloring Book

Step into Reading™ Books
Babar and the Ghost: An Easy-to-Read Version

This title was originally cataloged by the Library of Congress as follows: De Brunhoff, Jean   Babar the king; trans. from the French by Merle S. Haas. Random House c1935
unp col illus 1 Elephants—Stories 2 Picture books for children I. Title   E
ISBN 0-394-80580-1   0-394-90580-6 (lib. bdg.)

Off in the country of the elephants King Babar and Queen Celeste are rejoicing: they have signed a treaty of peace with the rhinoceros, and their friend, the Old Lady, has consented to remain with them. She often tells the elephants' children stories; her little monkey, Zephir, perched up in a tree, also listens.

Leaving the Old Lady with Queen Celeste, Babar has gone for a walk along the banks of a large lake with Cornelius, the oldest and wisest of all the elephants, and he says to him, "This countryside is so beautiful that I would like to see it every day

as I wake up. We must build our city here. Our houses shall be on the shores of the lake, and shall be surrounded with flowers and birds." Zephir, who has followed them, would like to catch a butterfly he sees . . . .

While chasing the butterfly, Zephir meets his friend
Arthur, the young cousin of the King and Queen, who
was amusing himself hunting for snails. All of a sudden
they see one, two, three, four dromedaries . . . five, six,
seven dromedaries . . . eight, nine, ten . . . . There are more
than they can count. And the chief of the cavalcade calls to
them: "Can you please tell us where we can find King
Babar?"

Escorted by Arthur and Zephir, the dromedaries have found Babar. They are bringing him all his heavy baggage and all the things which he had bought out in the big world, during his honeymoon. Babar thanks them: "You must be tired, gentlemen. Won't you rest under the shade of the palm trees?" Then, turning to the Old Lady and to Cornelius, he says: "Now we will be able to build our city."

Having called an assembly of all the elephants, Babar climbs up on a packing case and, in a loud voice, proclaims the following words: "My friends, I have in these trunks, these bales, and these sacks, gifts for each of you. There are dresses, suits, hats and materials, paint boxes, drums, fishing tackle and rods, ostrich feathers, tennis rackets and many other things. I will divide all this among you as soon as we have finished building our city. This city—the city of the elephants — I would like to suggest that we name Celesteville, in honor of your Queen."

All the elephants raised their trunks and cried: "What a good idea! What an excellent idea!"

The elephants set to work quickly. Arthur and Zephir hand out the tools. Babar tells each one what he should do. He marks with sign-boards where the streets and houses should go. He orders some to cut down trees, some to move stones; others saw wood or dig holes. With what joy they all strive to do their best! The Old Lady is playing the phonograph for them and from time to time Babar plays on his trumpet; he is fond of music. All the elephants are as happy as he is. They drive nails, draw logs, pull and push, dig, fetch and carry, opening their big ears wide as they work.

Over in the big lake the fish are complaining among themselves: "We can't even sleep peacefully any longer," they say. "These elephants make the most dreadful noise! What are they building? When we jump out of the water we really haven't time to see clearly. We'll have to ask the frogs what it is all about."

The birds also gathered together to discuss what the elephants were up to. The pelicans and the flamingos, the ducks and the ibis and even the smaller birds all twittered, chirruped and quacked, and the parrots enthusiastically kept repeating: "Come and see Celesteville, the most beautiful of all cities! Come and see Celesteville, the most beautiful of all cities!"

Here is Celesteville! The elephants have just finished building it and are resting or bathing. Babar goes for a sail with Arthur and Zephir. He is well satisfied, and admires his new capital. Each elephant has his own house. The Old Lady's is at the

upper left, the one for the King and Queen is at the upper right. The big lake is visible from all their windows. The Bureau of Industry is next door to the Amusement Hall which will be very practical and convenient.

Today Babar keeps his promise. He gives a gift to each elephant and also serviceable clothes suitable for work-days and beautiful rich clothes for holidays. After thanking their King most heartily, the elephants all go home dancing with glee.

Babar has decided that next Sunday all the elephants will
dress up in their best clothes and assemble in the gardens
of the Amusement Park. The gardeners have much to do.
They rake the paths, water the flower beds and set out the
last flower pots.

The elephant children are planning a surprise for Babar and Celeste. They have asked Cornelius to teach them the song of the elephants. Arthur had the idea. They are very attentive, keep time, and will know it perfectly by Sunday.

SONG OF THE ELEPHANTS

MELODY

Pa- ta- li di- ra- pa- ta crom- da crom- da ri- pa- lo

REFRAIN :

Pa- ta Pa- ta ko ko ko

WORDS

1st VERSE

PATALI DIRAPATA
CROMDA CROMDA RIPALO
PATA PATA
KO KO KO

2nd VERSE

BOKORO DIPOULITO
RONDI RONDI PEPINO
PATA PATA
KO KO KO

3rd VERSE

EMANA KARASSOLI
LOUCRA LOUCRA PONPONTO
PATA PATA
KO KO KO

NOTE: This song is the old chant of the Mammoths.
Cornelius himself doesn't know what the words mean —

The cooks are hurriedly preparing cakes and dainties of all kinds. Queen Celeste comes to help them. Zephir comes too, with Arthur. He tastes the vanilla cream to see if it is just right; first he puts in his finger, then his hand, and then his arm. Arthur is dying of envy and would like to stick his trunk in it.

In order to have one last taste Zephir bends his head, sticks out his tongue and *plouf!*—in he falls head first. At this sound the chief cook looks around and, greatly annoyed, fishes him out by the tail. The soup chef bursts out laughing. Arthur hides. Poor little Zephir is a sight, all yellow and sticky. Celeste scolds him and goes off to clean him up.

Sunday comes at last. In the gardens of the Amusement Park
the elephants saunter about dressed magnificently. The children
have sung their song, Babar has kissed each one. The cakes

were delicious! What a wonderful day! Unfortunately, it is
over all too soon. The Old Lady is already organizing the last
round of hide-and-seek.

The next day after their morning dip in the lake, the children go to school. And they are glad to find their dear teacher, the Old Lady, waiting for them. Lessons are never tiresome when she teaches.

After having settled the little ones at their tasks, she turns

her attention to the older ones, and asks them: "Two times two?" — "Three," answers Arthur. "No, no, four," said his neighbor Ottilie. "For, that's what we study for," sang Zephir. "Four," repeated Arthur. "I'll not forget that again, teacher."

All the elephants who are too old to attend classes, have chosen a trade. For example: Tapitor is a cobbler, Pilophage an officer, Capoulosse is a doctor, Barbacol a tailor, Podular a sculptor and Hatchibombotar is a street cleaner. Doulamor is a musician, Olur is a mechanic, Poutifour a farmer, Fandago is a learned man. Justinien is a painter and Coco a clown. If Capoulosse has holes in his shoes, he brings them to Tapitor, and, if Tapitor is sick, Capoulosse takes care of him. If Barbacol wants a statue for his mantelpiece, he asks Podular to carve one for him, and when Podular's coat is worn out Barbacol makes a new one to order for him. Justinien paints a portrait of Pilophage, who will protect him against his enemies. Hatchibombotar cleans the streets, Olur repairs the automobiles, and, when they are all tired, Doulamor plays his cello to entertain them. After having settled grave problems, Fandago relaxes and eats some of Poutifour's fruits. As for Coco, he keeps them all laughing and gay.

At Celesteville, all the elephants work in the morning, and in the afternoon they can do as they please. They play, go for walks, read and dream . . . . Babar and Celeste like to play tennis with Mr. and Mrs. Pilophage.

Cornelius, Fandago, Podular and Capoulosse prefer to play bowls. The children play with Coco, the clown. Arthur and Zephir have put on masks. There is a shallow pool in which to sail their boats and there are many other games besides.

But what the elephants like best of all

is the theater in the Amusement Park.

Every day, early in the morning, Hatchibombotar sprinkles the streets with his motor sprinkler. When Arthur and Zephir meet him, they quickly take off their shoes, and run after the car, barefoot. "Oh, what a fine shower!" they say laughingly. Unfortunately, Babar caught them at it one day. "No dessert for either of you, you rascals!" he cried.

Arthur and Zephir are mischievous, as are all little boys, but they are not lazy. Babar and Celeste visit the Old Lady, and are amazed to hear them play the violin and cello. "It is wonderful!" says Celeste, and Babar adds: "My dear children, I am indeed pleased with you. Go to the pastry shop and select whatever cakes you like."

Arthur and Zephir are very happy to have had all the
cakes they wanted, but they are even more delighted when
at the distribution of prizes, they hear Cornelius read out:
"First prize for music: a tie between Arthur and Zephir."
Very proudly, with wreaths on their heads, they went back
to their seats. After having rewarded the good scholars,
Cornelius made a noble speech.

". . . And now I wish you all a pleasant holiday!" he ended up. Everyone clapped hard and applauded loudly. Then, quite weary, he sat down, but alas and alack, his fine hat was on the chair and he crushed it completely. "A regular pancake!" said Zephir. Cornelius was aghast, and sadly looked at what was left of his hat. What would he wear on the next formal occasion?

The Old Lady promises Cornelius to sew some plumes on
his old derby, and in order to console him further, she
invites him to go for a ride on the new merry-go-round
which Babar has just had built.

Podular has carved the animals, Justinien has painted them, and the motor was installed by Olur. All three of them are very skillful. They have also made the King's mechanical horse. Olur has just oiled it and Babar is winding it up. He wants to give it a final trial before the big celebration on the anniversary of the founding of Celesteville.

The weather is perfect the day of the celebration. Arthur marches at the head of the parade with Zephir and the band. Cornelius follows, his hat

completely transformed. Then come the soldiers and the trades companies.
All those who are not marching are watching this unforgettable spectacle.

1 On his way home from the celebration Zephir notices a curious stick.

2 He goes to pick it up. Horrors! It is a snake which rears its head and hisses,

3 and cruelly bites the Old Lady who tries to hide Zephir in her arms.

4 Arthur furiously smashes his bugle on the snake's back and kills it.

The Old Lady's arm swells rapidly, and she hastens to the hospital.

Dr. Capoulosse takes care of her, and gives her a hypodermic of serum.

Zephir sadly remains near his mistress. She is very ill.

"I can't tell you until tomorrow whether she will get well," Capoulosse says to Babar.

As Babar leaves the hospital, he hears cries of "Fire! Fire!" Cornelius' house is on fire. The stairway is already full of smoke; the firemen succeed in rescuing Cornelius, but he is half suffocated and a burning beam has injured him. Capoulosse, summoned in great haste, gives him first-aid before having him moved to the hospital. A match which Cornelius thought he had thrown into the ashtray but which had actually fallen, still lighted, in the trashbasket, had been enough to start this terrible fire.

That night when Babar goes to bed, he shuts his eyes but cannot sleep. "What a dreadful day!" he thinks. "It began so well. Why did it have to end so badly? Before these two accidents we were all so happy and peaceful at Celesteville!

"We had forgotten that misfortune existed! Oh my dear old Cornelius, and you, dear Old Lady, I would give my crown to see you cured. Capoulosse was to telephone me any news. Oh! How long this night seems, and how worried I am!"

· ·

Babar finally drops off to sleep, but his sleep is restless and soon *he dreams:* He hears a knocking on his door. Tap! Tap! Tap! Then a voice says to him: "It is I, Misfortune, with some of my companions, come to pay you a visit." Babar looks out of the window, and sees a frightful old woman surrounded by flabby ugly beasts. He opens his mouth to shout: "Ugh! Faugh! Go away quickly!" But he stops to listen to a very faint noise — *Frr! Frr! Frr!* — as of birds flying in a flock, and he sees coming toward him . . .

. . . graceful winged elephants who
chase Misfortune away from Celesteville and bring back Happiness. At
this point he awakes, and feels ever
so much better.

GOODNESS

FEAR

DESPAIR

INDOLENCE

MISFORTUNE

SICKNESS

ANGER

STUPIDITY

DISCOURAGEMENT

Babar dresses and runs to the hospital. Oh joy! What does
he see? His two patients walking in the garden. He can
hardly believe his eyes. "We are all well again," says
Cornelius, "but all this excitement has made me as hungry
as a wolf. Let's get some breakfast, and then later we'll
rebuild my house."

A week later, in Babar's drawing room, the Old Lady says to her two friends: "Do you see how in this life one must never be discouraged? The vicious snake didn't kill me, and Cornelius is completely recovered. Let's work hard and cheerfully and we'll continue to be happy."

And since that day, over in the elephant's country, everyone has been happy and contented.